JiGGLE
WiGGLE
PRANCE
by Sally Noll

FOR TORY

The full-color art work,
gouache paintings, was
mechanically color-separated
and reproduced in
four colors.
The text typeface
is Avant Garde Bold.

Puffin Books

BOOKS   Published by the Penguin Group, Penguin Books USA Inc., 375 Hudson Street, New York, New York 10014, U.S.A.

uin Books Ltd, 27 Wrights Lane, London W8 5TZ, England • Penguin Books Australia Ltd, Ringwood, Victoria, Australia

in Books Canada Ltd, 10 Alcorn Avenue, Toronto, Ontario, Canada M4V 3B2

in Books (N.Z.) Ltd, 182–190 Wairau Road, Auckland 10, New Zealand

in Books Ltd, Registered Offices: Harmondsworth, Middlesex, England

ublished in the United States of America by Greenwillow Books, a division of William Morrow & Company, Inc., 1987

ted by arrangement with William Morrow & Company, Inc.   Published in Puffin Books, 1993

  8 7 6 5 4 3 2 1

ight © Sally Noll, 1987   All rights reserved

LIBRARY OF CONGRESS CATALOGING-IN-PUBLICATION DATA

Noll, Sally.   Jiggle, wiggle, prance / by Sally Noll.   p. cm.

Summary: Includes illustrations of animals acting out such rhyming action words as ''pull, flop, hop'' and
    ''dance, prance.''

ISBN 0-14-054883-1

1. English language—Rhyme—Juvenile literature.   2. English language–Verb–Juvenile literature.   [1. English

language—Rhyme.   2. Vocabulary.]   I. Title.

[PE1517.N6   1993]   428.1—dc20   92-25332

Printed in Hong Kong

WALK

ROCK DROP

PUSH

PULL **FLOP**

HOP

SPIN

DANCE

JIGGLE WIGGLE

PRANCE

FOLLOW FLY

SWING

HOBBLE

WOBBLE   FLING

JUMP

RUN RACE

SKIP **TRIP**

PACE

RIDE   DRIVE

ROLL

SKATE　　　　**STRIDE**

STROLL

CLIMB

SLIDE   FALL

AND THAT'S ALL.